Geronimo Stilton

MICEKINGS
ATTACK OF THE DRAGONS

Scholastic Inc.

Published by Scholastic Inc., 557 Broadway, New York, NY 10012. SCHOLASTIC and associated logos are trademarks and/or registered trademarks of Scholastic Inc.

Stilton is the name of a famous English cheese. It is a registered trademark of the Stilton Cheese Makers' Association. For more information, go to www. stiltoncheese.com.

ISBN 978-0-545-87238-6

Text by Geronimo Stilton
Original title *Sei ciccia per draghi!*
Cover by Giuseppe Facciotto (pencils) and Flavio Ferron (ink and color)
Illustrations by Giuseppe Facciotto (pencils) and Alessandro Costa (ink and color)
Graphics by Chiara Cebraro

Special thanks to Tracey West
Translated by Emily Clement
Interior design by Kay Petronio

10 9 8 7 6 5 4 3 2 1   16 17 18 19 20

Printed in the U.S.A.   40
First printing 2016

AHH, MICEKING WINTER!

It was an **ICY** winter morning in Mouseborg, the capital of Miceking Island. Snow covered the entire village, ice dangled from every roof, and the **freezing** north wind blew so **COLD** that my tail nearly turned into an icicle and fell off!

Winter here is truly shivery!

Excuse me — I haven't introduced myself yet. My name is *GERONIMO STILTONORD*, and I am a mouseking!

As I was saying, in **MOUSEBORG** the winter is very cold, but it's also the most peaceful time of year.

Why? The answer is simple: **DRAGONS** hate the winter! They are fiery beasts, and the cold and snow cools them down. So these enormouse, **hungry** creatures leave us micekings alone for a few months.

Ah, winter! What a fabumouse season!

Back to that wintry morning. I was snoring under a wool blanket in my cozy bed when a tremendous noise suddenly awakened me.

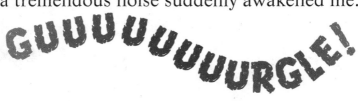

GUUUUUUUURGLE!

"Huh? Who said that?" I yelled.

My whiskers curled in fear, but then I heard the noise again.

GUUUUUUUURGLE!

The sound was coming from . . . my STOMACH! It was complaining because I hadn't had breakfast yet.

Still in my pajamas, I DRAGGED myself to the window, yawning like a bear coming out of hibernation. I PEERED outside.

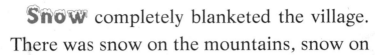

Snow completely blanketed the village. There was snow on the mountains, snow on the houses, and snow on the roads.

I was looking forward to spending the day in my **warm** little house.

"I'll start with a breakfast fit for a barbarian!" I announced.

I decided to make a pile of **toast** with two sticks of goat butter, a wedge of stinky **Stenchberg cheese**, a pan of **scrambled** seagull eggs, and a big wild blueberry smoothie. I wanted to keep it light, so I figured I would leave out the fjordberry jam.

Licking my lips in anticipation, I opened my cupboard and . . .

Great groaning glaciers!

The bread was . . . gone! The goat butter was . . . gone! The eggs, the stinky Stenchberg cheese, the wild blueberries . . . **ALL GONE!**

My cupboard was as EMPTY as a groundhog's den in spring. There wasn't even a piece of pickled seaweed left!

THE SPECIALTIES OF MICEKING COOKING

We micekings have a true passion for the fish of the cold north seas. We also love CHEESE, of course!

What a smell!

1

An ancient miceking saying is: CHEESE IS LIKE FISH — THE STINKIER THE BETTER!

In fact, STENCHBERG CHEESE (1), one of the most prized miceking cheeses, has an odor that will make you collapse from a thousand tails away!

Slurp!

2

For dessert we love herring ice cream topped with melted goat cheese, and PIE made with fjordberry jam and seaweed (2). It's delicious!

Tasty!

During grand miceking feasts, we drink FINNBREW (3), made of equal parts codfish juice and herring juice, with a splash of squid ink.

3

But the greatest MICEKING SPECIALTY of all is a stew called GLOOG (4). Included in the ingredients are herring scales, crab claws, melted Stenchberg cheese, and seagull eggs. Mousehilde, the wife of our village chief, makes the best gloog anywhere — but her complete recipe is a secret!

4

Get in line!

I sighed. **"But** . . . **but** . . . how can this be?"

Then it hit me . . . how long had it been since I'd gone shopping? Squeak! It was so cold that I had kept putting it off.

GUUUUUUUURGLE!

Oh no! My stomach was complaining again. There was only one solution: I had to go outside and get supplies. But that meant facing the icy north wind. **BRRRRRRRRRR!** Just thinking about it made my whiskers shiver!

GUUURGLE!
GUUUUUUUURGLE!

To go out in that cold, I had to put on **three** thick tunics, **two** wool coats, gloves, and fur earmuffs.

I was so busy bundling up that I forgot to take off my **PAJAMAS** first! So I had to start all over again.

When I was finally ready, I staggered to the door, timidly opened it, and . . .

SWOOOOOOOOSH!

An icy gust of wind curled my whiskers.

Shivering squids! It was barbarically chilly!

I plodded through the snow, pushing against the *icy wind* to get to the

marketplace.
As I got closer,
the smell of
Stenchberg cheese
TICKLED my nose.

I sniffed the air, enjoying the
delicious aroma, when . . .

GUUUUUUUURGLE!

Great groaning
glaciers, I was so
hungry!

How embarrassing! Luckily, there was no one around. At least, that's what I thought.

Suddenly, a big, heavy rodent **SKIDDED** down the hill and banged right into me!

"DRAAAAAGON ALERT!

Take **cover**, Geronimo! Do you hear those **terrifying** cries? It's dragons. We're under attack!"

It was my cousin Trap! **"DR-DR-DRAGONS?"** I stammered. "Are you sure?"

Trap ducked behind a mound of snow and **looked** up at the sky.

Just then . . .

GUUUUUUURGLE!

My stomach rumbled once again! How **embarrassing**!

I **blushed**, and then explained to Trap, "Sorry, Cousin. I haven't had breakfast yet, and my empty stomach is making some Little noises. Could you perhaps, er, have mistaken it for the roar of a DRAGON?"

Trap looked at me sternly. "What kind of JOKE is that, Geronimo? You shouldn't fool rodents with a false dragon alert! That's just not funny."

"It wasn't a prank," I protested. "I'm SORRY!"

Trap nodded. "I accept your apology, Geronimo. And now you can repay me by **testing** my new invention: the ratsled!"

I noticed that he had a large bundle strapped to his back. I could see WOODEN boards, hooks, and oiled rope sticking out. That looked dangerous!

I shook my head. "Forget it, Trap. Every time I test one of your **INVENTIONS**, I risk my fur!"

"You're **exaggerating**, Geronimo," Trap said. "This is totally safe. You'll see — by the end of the test run, you'll want to do it all over again!"

I sighed. Trap can be as **STUBBORN** as a mountain. He won't take no for an answer!

A **GUST** of wind hit me, and I **shivered**. I supposed that anything would be better than standing around **FREEZING**!

"All right, I'll do it," I squeaked. "But first, I must eat **breakfast**!"

Trap took me by the arm and nodded

happily. "Of course! I wouldn't deny the last wish of my **best tester**!"

"Last wish?" I squeaked.

Let's go, Cousin!

MICEKING TRAINING

On the road, Trap and I ran into **Sven the Shouter**, the village chief, followed by a line of micekings in training gear. They were singing the miceking training anthem.

"WE TRAIN HARD ALL DAY LONG! WE FIGHT AND KICK AND SWING! WE ARE BRAVE AND WE ARE STRONG, FOR WE ARE THE MICEKINGS!"

No matter how cold it is outside, micekings must train every day.

Why don't I train with the micekings? I am what's known as a **SMARTY-MOUSEKING**.

SVEN
The Shouter

Sven is the leader of our village. All of Mouseborg admires and respects him. He's called "the Shouter" because he shouts louder than anyone, and he shouts all the time. Mostly, he shouts AT ME! He cannot understand why I have never earned a miceking helmet, our greatest honor.

I am all brains and no muscles. I hid behind a tree, and tried to make myself look very, very SMALL, hoping they wouldn't see me.

But **SVEN** the Shouter spotted me. "Geronimo, you good-for-nothing smarty-mouseking! Are you hiding?"

"N-no, I'm not," I nervously replied. "I was, um, just looking for my notepad."

"A notepad won't help you train on the Field of Eternal

Challenges. You need muscles! And since you're as soft as a jellyfish, it's time to train. Let's go!"

I sighed. "But I'm hungry! I didn't eat breakfast."

But **Sven the Shouter** didn't care about my breakfast. He shouted at me, "SMARTY-MOUSEKING, no excuses! Get moving and train until I can see one little muscle pop up on your scrawny arm. So says Sven the Shouter!"

"SO SAYS SVEN THE SHOUTER!"

echoed the other micekings in a loud roar.

Trap and I marched with them to the Field of Eternal Challenges, where I began my miceking training.

I was **not** cut out for that kind of exercise!

Oof!

MICEKING PUSH-UPS

First I had to do three hundred **PUSH-UPS** on only one paw! I'm not even good at push-ups using **both** paws.

After doing only two, my stomach rumbled loudly.

GUUUUUUUURGLE!

The micekings began to shout, "Look out! Dragons!"

Trap snickered. "Hee, hee. Relax! It's just my cousin's stomach."

Sven turned **red** with rage. "Geronimo, lift up that pile of **logs** . . . with your

Oops!

WHISKER LIFTS

whiskers!" he demanded.

I quickly attached the logs to my whiskers, and my stomach started to complain again.

GUUUUUUUURGLE!

The other micekings dropped to the ground. "Take cover! **Dragon alert!**"

Trap giggled. "Relax! It's just Geronimo again."

Sven grumbled. "Hey you, jellyfish legs!" he called out to me. "Stop interrupting our practice. Get over there and toss some BOULDERS.

Uh-oh!

BOULDER TOSS

So says Sven the Shouter!"

The micekings echoed him:

"SO SAYS SVEN THE SHOUTER!"

I trudged over to the boulders. I hoped to find one that fit in the palm of my paw. But the SMALLEST boulder weighed more than I did . . . clothes included!

I was so **worn out**!

I didn't have enough energy to lift a crumb of cheese. But I tried to lift the boulder anyway. My stomach roared loudly.

GUUUUUUUURGLE!

The micekings started zigzagging around in terror.

"THE DRAGONS ARE COMING!"
they screamed.

Sven the Shouter fumed with anger. "Great groaning glaciers, that's ENOUGH! Go eat some gloog, Geronimo. That's an order!"

"Y-yes, Sven," I stammered.

Sven turned to the micekings. "We're taking a break so that Geronimo won't be bothering us with his rumbling stomach anymore!"

I blushed. How embarrassing!

But I wasn't too upset. I was hungry enough to eat a MOUNTAIN of gloog!

"Everyone, march to my house!" Sven ordered.

ACHOO! ACHOO!

By the time we reached Sven's house, all of us were as hungry as **BEARS** coming out of hibernation.

"**Mousehilde!** I brought some guests," Sven called out. "Can you make your famouse **gloog** for them?"

As you know by now, every rodent in Mouseborg loves gloog. And in all the *Lands of the North*, there is no gloog as delicious as Mousehilde's. She follows a **SECRET** recipe that the micekings in her family have passed down for centuries!

But we did not **see** Mousehilde anywhere. And the only thing on the kitchen table was an **EMPTY** stew pot!

"Wife, where are you?" Sven called out. Then he frowned. "**THORA!**"

A moment later the most *beautiful* mouseking in the village stepped into the kitchen. It was Thora, Sven's daughter. Her eyes were as blue as the **water** of the fjord,* and her hair was as red as the sunset. She was also the most athletic, intelligent, and courageous mouseking I had ever met. What a **wonderful** rodent!

Hi!

"**Lower** your voice, Papa," Thora said in a whisper. She pointed to a pile of blankets in the corner. "Mama isn't well."

* A *fjord* is a long, narrow ocean cove between cliffs.

"Aaa-achoo! Achoo!"

Mousehilde sneezed from under the blankets. Sven rushed to her side. "Wife, what is wrong?" he asked.

"Achoo! Aaa-achoo!"

"She has a barbaric cold," explained Thora. Sven looked worried. "What can I do to make it better?"

"She needs rest and warmth," Thora replied. "But what would really help is a hot cup of wild mint tea. It's the perfect cure, passed down from my grandmother's grandmother's grandmother."

Sven scoffed. "Wild mint tea? Pah! We'll take your mother to Loki Longsight!"

Mousehilde spoke up in a hoarse voice. "Why do I need a fortune-teller? I only have a little cold. Achoo!"

The whole house **ROCKED** from Mousehilde's sneeze!

"Longsight knows the art of healing with herbs," Sven said. "And I am taking you to see him. That's an *order*!"

When Sven shouts an order, no rodent dares disobey him.

"SO SAYS SVEN THE SHOUTER!"

cried the micekings.

THIS CALLS FOR MINT TEA!

We all headed to Loki Longsight's **CAVE**. Mousehilde, supported by Sven, continued to sneeze and cough.

"Achoo! Aaa-achoo!"

Sven pounded on the door. "Loki Longsight, you good-for-nothing fortune-teller! Open up! That's an order!"

SO SAYS SVEN THE SHOUTER!

cried the micekings.

The door didn't open. Then a **STONE** came flying through a slot in the door.

The stone hit me right in the paw. **Ouch!**

Then I noticed a piece of parchment tied around it.

"*GERONIMO*, you're as **weak** as a baby herring. But you're a **SMARTY-MOUSEKING**, so read it to us!" Sven ordered.

I read out loud: *"The fortune-teller will answer many questions . . . but only during the full moon! If it's not raining! Each answer costs one wheel of Stenchberg cheese."*

There was more on the other side of the parchment.

"*Buy five answers, get one free.* **Payment due in advance!**"

Sven turned bright **RED**. "Loki Longsight! This is an **emergency**! Mousehilde needs to get better right away, so she can make us all some **gloog**!"

After that outburst, the fortune-teller threw **another** stone with parchment tied to it. Then **another**, then **ANOTHER**, and **another**! I quickly gathered them up, reading the messages.

"*What symptoms does the patient have? Spots on her nose? Red ears? A green face? Flat fur?*"

Mousehilde looked insulted,

but before she could say anything she sneezed again.

"Achoo! Aaa-achoo!"

"These are her symptoms," I called out. "Sneezing, coughing, and a nose running like a **raging river**!"

The slot opened up again and another **STONE** flew out.

*"The fortune-teller has reached an answer: The patient has a **miceking cold**! She just needs a little rest and a double layer of wool blankets. Now please pay the fortune-teller."*

Sven started **SHOUTING** again. "Loki Longsight, you codfish face! We can't **wait** for this cold to pass on its own."

He pounded on the door. "We need a *fast* cure, now! So says Sven the Shouter!"

"SO SAYS SVEN THE SHOUTER!"

echoed the micekings.

Another note came through the slot.

"**SMARTY-MOUSEKING**, what does it say?" Sven asked.

"He says to give him a minute," I replied.

Sven frowned, but another note **flew out** a minute later.

> If you need to cure a cold,
> and you need to do it quickly,
> there is one cure to be told:
> Drink some wild mint tea!

As soon as she heard this, Mousehilde flung her **rolling pin** at her husband.

"You should have listened to your daughter!" she said. "Thora already told you that her **grandmother's grandmother's grandmother's** remedy was the best!"

Sven shrugged. "Fine, then!" he growled. "Thora, run and make some tea for your mother."

"You don't understand!" said Mousehilde. "Thora can't — *Achoo!*"

WILD MINT

TASTE: As icy fresh as a glacier! One sniff will clear your nostrils.

USE: It adds flavor to any food, and the micekings believe it cures a cold.

CHARACTERISTICS: It grows only in the warm summer months. It can be dried to use in winter, but doesn't last long when there's a bad cold season!

Mousehilde wiped her nose. "She can't make WILD mint tea," she continued. "Aaa-choo!"

"What do you mean? Sven the Shouter has ordered it!" her husband said.

"I know, I know," Mousehilde replied. "But wild mint is a summer plant. Achoo! It's been a bad cold season and all of the dried mint in the village is gone. Achoo!"

BRING YOUR
TRAVEL BAG!

Sven **frowned**. "This can't be true. There must be some wild mint somewhere!"

Then he **questioned** all of the micekings to try to locate some.

"I just finished mine yesterday!"

"Last week!"

"Last month!"

Sven interrupted them. "Enough, you fools! This is an **EMERGENCY**!"

Just then, another **STONE** wrapped in parchment flew out of the slot in the door. I picked it up and quickly read it. Then I **TUGGED** on Sven's cape.

"Chief, I have to tell you something," I said.

"**LATER**, Geronimo," he said. "Can't you see I'm busy?"

But I couldn't give up. "Excuse me, but it's really *important*!"

Um, Chief?

Silence!

"Geronimo, I have NO TIME to chat with a smarty-mouseking!" Sven roared. "I have a **SERIOUS PROBLEM**: finding some wild mint. Do you know where to find some, you sniveling shrimp?"

I faltered. "I . . . I . . . I . . . no, but Loki Longsight does!"

Sven exploded. "Why didn't you say so, **JELLYFISH BRAINS**? Tell us everything! Read us the note!"

I obeyed. "According to the fortune-teller, there's only one place where **wild mint** grows in winter: the sulfurous springs* at the summit of Eagles' Cliff."

"**Great groaning glaciers**, there's not a minute to waste!" Sven cried. "We need to leave immediately!"

"We're ready, **CHief**!" the micekings

---

* The sulfurous springs contain sulfurous water, which comes out of the ground hot and smells like rotten eggs — which is why dragons love it!

shouted. Everyone was volunteering to go — that is, everyone except me!

"I don't need all of you," Sven said, and he turned to me. "Geronimo, since you are the **SMARTY-MOUSEKING** in our village, you will go — even though *you're as soft as a fish fillet*! Your cousin Trap will also go, since he's already wearing his travel pack. And since I don't really trust you two, your sister, **THEA**, will come, too. She will surely recognize the right plant."

I was paralyzed with fear. "But . . . but . . . but . . . I still haven't had *BREAKFAST*! I have to say good-bye to my nephew Benjamin. And I don't have a bag packed!"

"**Save** your excuses, **SMARTY-MOUSEKING**!" Sven boomed. "You will leave now, and that's an order!"

"SO SAYS SVEN THE SHOUTER!"

the micekings cried.

Sven started shouting again. "Thooooora! Bring your travel bag for Geronimo!"

Then I knew I couldn't refuse to go any longer. What would the brave **Thora** think of me? I hoisted her travel bag onto my back. Oof! It weighed as much as a **MOUNTAIN**!

Sven started shouting again.

"Quick! To the dock!" he ordered. "Olaf will take you on his drekar. And Geronimo, if you are successful, there might be a **miceking helmet** for you!"

As soon as Olaf and his **smelly** ship were mentioned, my whiskers began to tremble with anxiety. I had traveled with him before, and it had been a disaster. But there was nothing to do about it. Sven had made his *decision*! And who knows — maybe I would earn a miceking helmet!

TRAP and I went to the dock. Thea was waiting for us in front of Olaf's drekar — his miceking boat. He called it *Bated Breath*.

"Where have you been?" Olaf asked as soon as we arrived. "The sea is starting to **freeze** over. We must leave!"

"Couldn't I nibble on some cheese

before we go?" I asked.

"**Shivering squids!** Do you think you're going on a cruise?" Olaf thundered. "Get yourself **ON BOARD** before I do it for you!"

Not Olaf's drekar!

We're here!

Hurry up and get on board!

You Slipped, Geronimo!

I climbed on board and dropped my travel pack, and Olaf **pawed** me an ice ax. He pointed to a shaky wooden swing hanging from the dragon-shaped **figurehead*** at the front of the ship.

"Climb on there, **blubberhead**!" he ordered me. "Use your puny muscles to chop away the ice in the water as it forms."

"But captain, I get drekar-sick, and I'm **afraid** of heights!" I protested.

"Tough!" Olaf said. "We'll **sink** if you don't take care of the ice!"

"B-b-but —" I stammered.

---

* A *figurehead* is a sculpture that decorates the front of a ship.

"No buts!" Olaf yelled. "Get in that swing or I'll toss you in the sea! On the honor of Olaf the Fearless!"

Resigned to my task, I climbed out onto the swing that hung just above the water.

I got drekar-sick right away!

First I turned as **pale** as MOZZARELLA.

Then I turned as **GREEN** as **moldy** cheese.

And the gusts of **icy** wind practically turned me into a **frozen fish**!

We sailed up the coast toward Eagles' Cliff, but we didn't get far.

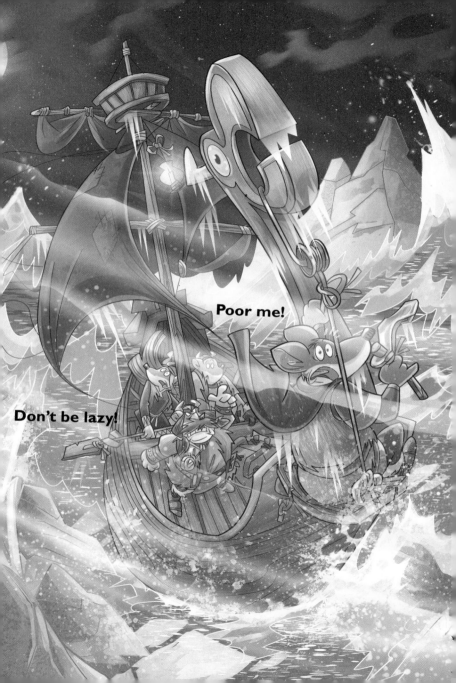

"The ice is too **thick**! We can't sail any farther," Olaf declared. "There's only one way to continue. By paw!" Then he laughed. "And you should get moving, unless you want to get TRAPPED in the ice until spring!"

Great groaning glaciers! Walking on the iced-over sea wasn't going to be easy. I MANAGED to take

steps . . . and then I slipped and fell on my back! SQUEAK!

I tried to stand up and slipped again, landing on my tail. Oww!

"Don't worry, Cousin," Trap said. "I have just what you need!"

He dug into his big **bag** and started to take out the strangest things: a compass, a **WHEEL**, some spicy cheese sticks . . .

"Hmm, I was sure I brought them," he muttered. "Maybe they're down at the **bottom**."

I sighed. "If it's another one of your **INVENTIONS**, I don't have any intention of testing it!" I told him.

Then he smiled. "Found them!"

He pulled out what **LOOKED** like two **METAL** pot lids with straps attached.

"What are you going to do with those?" Thea asked.

"Just trust me!" Trap said.

I wasn't sure what to **THINK**. He had me strap the lids to my **feet**, but I was confused.

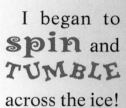

What . . .

1

I tried to take a step, but the lids did not **GRIP** the ice at all.

2

Oops!

I began to **spin** and **TUMBLE** across the ice!

Help . . .

3

I was spinning in **circles**! Trap and Thea clapped for me.

WHIIIRRRR

Then, with a final tumble, I slipped and landed right on my snout. Brrr, how icy!

"**HOORAY**, Cousin!" Trap cheered. "That was some pretty **FANCY FOOTWORK** out there."

Ow, ow, ow!

THE FOREST OF A THOUSAND SCALES

Between **TUMBLES**, we finally reached the shore, and I took off those **terrible** pot lids. But now there was a long trek ahead of us!

Thea walked past me, as *quick* and *nimble* as a reindeer.

"Come on, Geronimo. I know you're a smarty-mouseking, but you need to keep up!" she urged.

I plodded along, out of breath. "Pant . . . I'm not . . . **puff** . . . used to walking . . . **oof** . . . in the snow."

"Just breathe in the FRESH AIR!" she said. "Forward we go!"

Finally, we reached the **EDGE** of the FOREST OF A THOUSAND SCALES, an ancient, thick, and dangerous forest! We had barely taken a step under the snowy branches when the strong *gusts* of wind stopped and a deep silence fell over us.

What a **CREEPY** place!

Suddenly . . .

GUUUUUUUURGLE!

My stomach's roar echoed through the forest.

"**SHH! QUIET!**" Thea warned me, pointing to the trees.

I looked and saw a **red** bird with a **long** beak,

sleeping **peacefully**.

I moved closer to get a better look, when . . .

GUUUUUUURGLE!

Oh no! Not again!

The rumble of my stomach woke up the cute bird with a start.

"Don't just stand there like a **DRIED ANCHOVY**!" Thea called out. "Run, Geronimo!"

"*Move it*, Cousin!" Trap added.

I looked at them, confused. "Why should I run? It's just a **sweet**,

Wh-what's wrong?

harmless little bird."

The bird turned and looked at me with sleepy, **threatening** eyes.

Great groaning glaciers!

"That's a **blitzer**, and they don't like being woken up!" Thea explained. She knows a lot about animals. "Stay away from its **beak**, Geronimo!"

Suddenly, my stomach roared again.

GUUUUUUUURGLE!

Trap panicked. "Quick! An entire colony

of blitzers lives here. We don't want to wake them all up. Run!"

We **SCAMPERED** off as fast as a snow leopard — or at least, Trap and Thea did. I am not as *FAST* as they are, so the blitzer **dive-bombed** my head! Then it **PECKED** at me with its pointy beak!

Ow! Ow! Owieeeeeee!

Run!

Hurry!

PECK

PECK

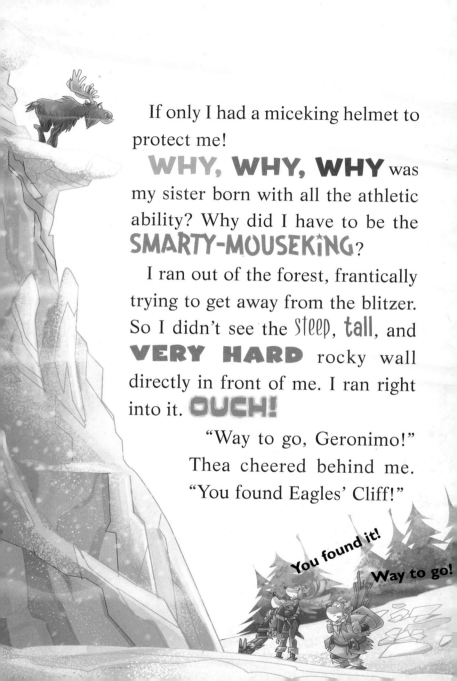

If only I had a miceking helmet to protect me!

WHY, WHY, WHY was my sister born with all the athletic ability? Why did I have to be the **SMARTY-MOUSEKiNG**?

I ran out of the forest, frantically trying to get away from the blitzer. So I didn't see the Steep, **tall**, and **VERY HARD** rocky wall directly in front of me. I ran right into it. **OUCH!**

"Way to go, Geronimo!" Thea cheered behind me. "You found Eagles' Cliff!"

You found it!

Way to go!

OH, DEER!

I gazed **UP** at the high, rocky wall of Eagles' Cliff.

"Do we really have to climb to the **very, very top**?" I asked. "I still haven't had breakfast!"

"We're so close, Geronimo," Thea said. "We'll get the wild mint, **climb** back down, and get you some food."

I was about to reply when . . .

GUUUUUUUURGLE!

Shivering squids, my stomach was getting louder each time! And **then** . . .

BOOOOOOOOOOOMMMM!

A deep rumble rang out from way up high. It sounded just like the **rumble** of my stomach . . . but **MUCH** louder!

"It wasn't me this time!" I said quickly before Trap could blame it on me.

Thea smiled. "It's just an **ECHO**, Geronimo. Now save your **BREATH**. You're going to need it!"

She was right. The climb was exhausting!

Over the next few hours we **walked** and **walked** and **walked** through the snow and cold.

Then, suddenly, I had a little **accident** as I tried to climb a very steep part of the **ROCKY** wall.

1 I slipped on the ice!

2 So I lost my grip and **fell** . . .

3 But luckily I got **SNAGGED** on Trap's backpack!

I climbed up again with the wind blowing in my face, FREEZING my ears and my paws.

Brrr! It was barbarically cold!

Finally, I reached the top — and saw a fjordberry bush with three large berries!

"Finally, some food!" I cried, DROOLING.

But I wasn't the ONLY

one who noticed the **berries**. A
REINDEER stepped up to the bush,
sniffing it. When it saw me, it began to
SCRAPE the ground with one hoof and
watch me with angry eyes.

Thea **slowly** inched toward me. "Don't
move, Geronimo! Leave it to me!"

My sister began to **gently** pet the
reindeer. It seemed to calm down — until it
noticed me reaching for the JUICY berries. I
couldn't help it! I was as hungry as a dragon!

Uh-oh!

BONK!

Ignoring Thea, the reindeer charged toward me and hit me with a **HEAD BUTT**.

Then the reindeer ate all of the **berries** right in front of my eyes!

I stood up, brushed off the **snow**, and then realized that the head butt had put me right in front of the entrance to a cave.

Heeeeelp!

Nice flight!

Thea sniffed the air. "We must be near the hot springs, where the wild mint grows. Do you smell the sulfur in the air, Geronimo?"

I nodded, distracted by a STRANGE SOUND I could hear coming from inside the cave. It sounded like the beating of wings.

Great groaning glaciers! Someone — or something — was inside that cave!

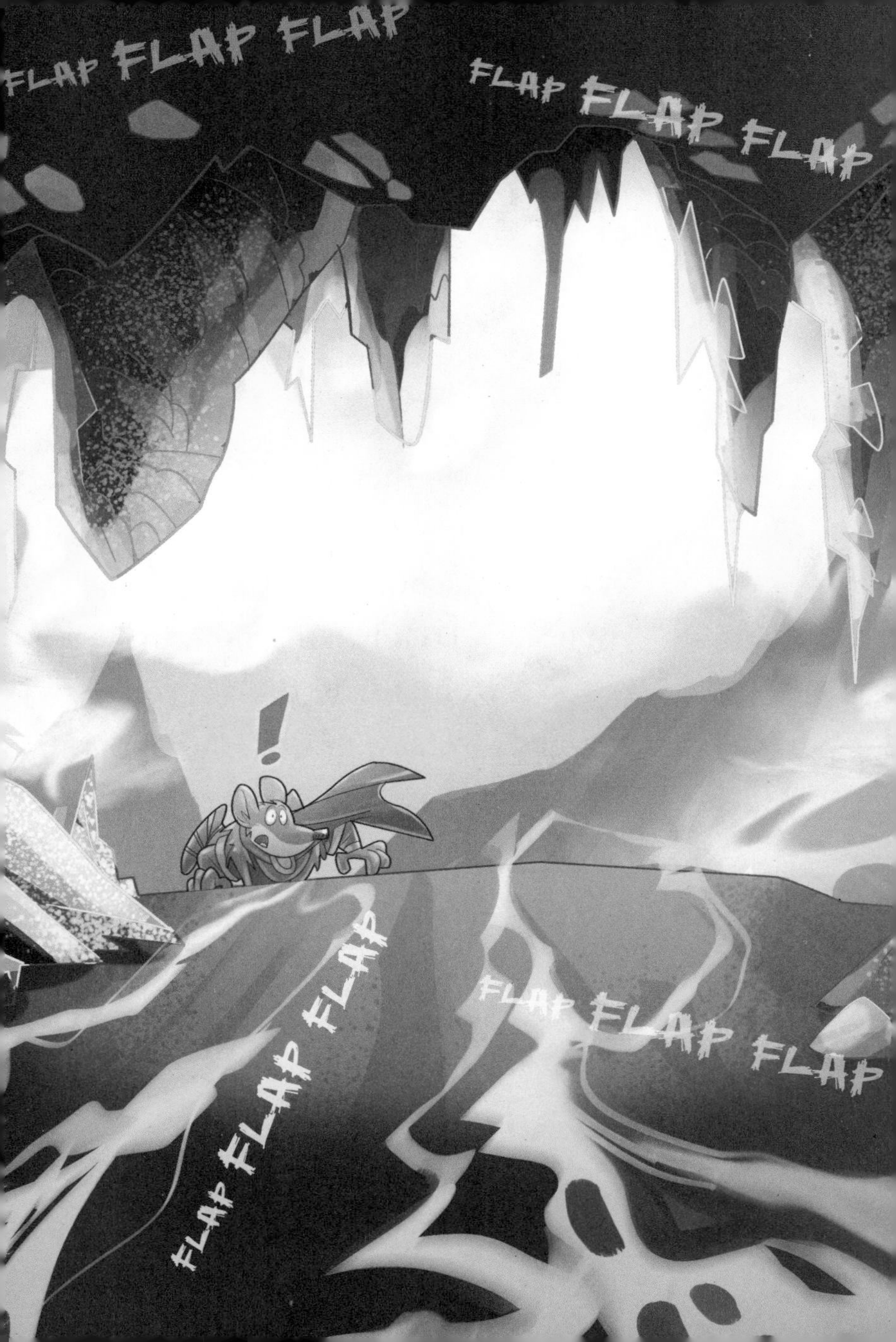
FLAP FLAP FLAP
FLAP FLAP FLAP
!
FLAP FLAP FLAP
FLAP FLAP FLAP

A Five-Star Cave

"I heard a **NOISE** in there," I told Thea and Trap, but they pushed past me.

"Probably another echo," Thea said. "Come on, let's find that wild mint!"

We went in. Everywhere we looked, we saw **smelly** pools of boiling, YELLOW sludge.

"It stinks in here!" Trap complained, holding his nose.

Once again, I heard the **strange** sound of wings.

"Didn't you hear that?" I asked. The fur on the back of my neck was standing up.

But Trap and Thea ignored me, determined to find the **wild mint**.

Suddenly, they both stopped short in front of me. I peered around them and my heart **JUMPED** into my throat.

Three **ENORMOUSE DRAGONS** were bathing in a stinky pool!

I recognized one of them: Sizzle, the terrible dragon cook from **Beastgard**,

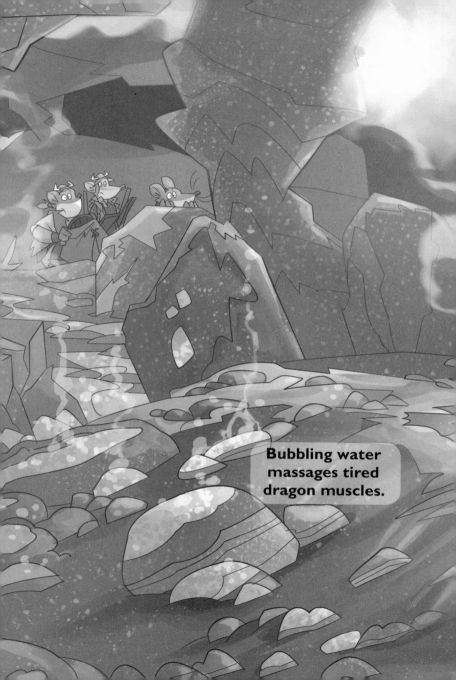

Bubbling water massages tired dragon muscles.

THE CAVE OF EAGLES' CLIFF

Hot sulfurous water makes for an invigorating shower.

How delightful!

How relaxing!

How peaceful!

Sulfur powder brightens tired scales.

SIZZLE
The Cook

Sizzle is the cook for the court of Gobbler the Putrid, the king of the dragons. Sizzle keeps rowdy dragons in line with his copper soup ladle. He rules the Dragon Kitchen, where he prepares tasty dishes — mostly made from miceking meat!

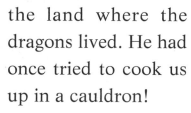

the land where the dragons lived. He had once tried to cook us up in a cauldron!

What was Sizzle doing here? And who were the other two?

"This **SSS**ulfurou**SSS** water ma**SS**age is truly **SSS**uperb, Chomper!" the orange dragon said.

Chomper rolled **OVER** on the ground. "And thi**SS** marvelou**SSSS** powder makes my **SSS**cales **SSS**o **S**hiny, Bully!" added the purple dragon.

"I alway**sss** keep my promi**sss**e**s**!" said Sizzle. His laugh echoed throughout the **cavern**.

"Tell u**sss**, how did you convince Gobbler, our king, to give you time off?" asked Bully.

Sizzle puffed up his scaly chest. "I earned thi**sss** vacation! I am the be**sss**t cook in Bea**s**tgard!"

"Three cheer**s** for **sss**izzle, who brought u**sss** along on hi**s** vacation!" growled

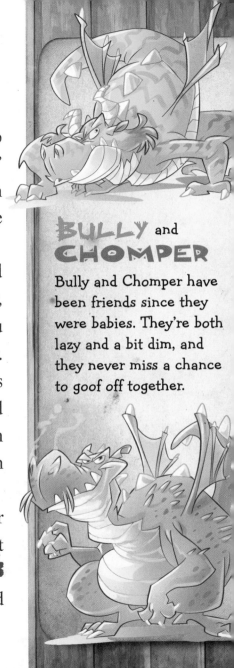

BULLY and **CHOMPER**

Bully and Chomper have been friends since they were babies. They're both lazy and a bit dim, and they never miss a chance to goof off together.

Bully and Chomper.

Thea nudged me. "**LOOK** over there! It's wild mint!" she whispered.

Through the clouds of STEAM, my sister had noticed some **green plants** growing between the rocks.

"How are we supposed to get it? If we get too close, the dragons will **SMELL** us!" I said.

Thea grinned. "Not if we cover ourselves in stinky slime!"

She gathered a pawful of the **smelly sludge** and started to smear it all over herself. Trap did the same. The slime smelled like ancient **rotten eggs**!

But the thought of the dragons was even **worse** than the smell. "I'll just stay behind," I said. "I can't mess up this new cloak that Benjamin just gave me. And I have an **urgent** appointment back in Mouseborg. Very, very **URGENT**!"

But before I could make another excuse, Trap splashed me with **sludge** from the top of my fur to the tip of my tail. Then he **pushed** me in front of him.

"That's our Geronimo, always **FIRST IN LINE**!" Trap said.

Here's some stinky slime!

FAREWELL, MY DEAR THORA!

My whiskers were trembling as we slipped past the DRAGONS, staying close to the cave walls. As we got closer to the wild mint plants, I could hear SIZZLE and his companions talking. Their conversation made my FUR stand on end!

Sizzle let out a sad sigh.

"If only I had a ta**SSS**ty fresh mou**SSS**eking," he said. "I would prepare a nice **SSS**nack!"

Chomper scratched his back against a boulder. "I prefer my miceking meat raw," he said, "**SSS**erved with a little **SSS**plash of lemon juice. Do you know how to make it that way, **SSS**izzle?"

"Of cour**SSS**e I know how to make it!" Sizzle replied.

I can cook anything!

"Can you make *grilled* miceking, cooked with lot**SSS** of fresh herb**SSS**?" Bully asked the cook.

Sizzle exploded into a laugh that shook the entire cave. "Ha, ha, ha! I **SSS**ee that you know nothing about cooking. A true cook like me know**SSS** that tho**S**e are all **SSS**ummer recipes! In the *winter*, you make miceking meat into a **SSS**tew!"

"Is miceking **SSS**tew ta**SSS**ty?" asked Chomper.

Sizzle shook his soup ladle in the air. "You mu**SSS**t cook the mou**SSS**eking over low heat all night, **SSS**o that it will ab**SSS**orb the flavor**SSS** of the **SSS**pices!" he said, licking his lips.

My body went as limp as MELTED CHEESE. I was too TERRIFIED to take another step!

But Thea had just reached the *wild mint* plants.

She gathered a few sprigs and **STUFFED** them in her bag. A moment later, Trap followed her and put some more wild mint into his pack.

I was left behind, alone and **paralyzed** with fear!

Suddenly . . .

GUUUURGLE!

Oops!

GUUUURGLE

The loud roaring of my stomach **echoed** throughout the cave! Then it grew silent.

The **DRAGONS** whipped around, and . . . **SURPRISED** Thea and Trap next to the **wild mint**!

Sizzle blocked their way, waving his soup ladle. "Fresh miceking meat! What a nice **SSS**urpri**S**e!"

Bully let out a cheer. "What luck! Let'**SSS** cook them up for **SSS**upper!"

I was frozen in **FEAR**. I thought the dragons hadn't seen me — but then Chomper **SPOtted** me from the corner of his eye. To my surprise, he quickly **HID ME** behind his long tail.

"**SSS**tay quiet," he whispered to me, licking his **fangs**. "I'll **SSS**lurp you up later **SSS**o I don't have to share your ta**SSS**ty chop**S** with anyone."

This is the end! I thought. *Farewell, my dear Thora!*

Meanwhile, SIZZLE had tied up poor Trap and Thea.

Sizzle was just about to drop Trap and Thea into a STEAMING POOL

when Bully stopped him with a yell.

"**SSS**top! Who **SSS**ay**S** they **S**hould be boiled? I want them roa**SSS**ted! Let me cook them over those red-hot rock**SSS** over there!"

"**I** am the king'**SSS** cook!" Sizzle fumed. "**I** decide how to cook miceking**SSS**!"

Chomper chimed in. "**SSS**o what? Thi**SSS** i**S**n't the king'**SSS** court."

Sizzle did not back down. "Thi**SSS** is my vacation, remember? I ju**SSS**t brought you two lo**S**er**SSS** along with me. **SSS**o I'm going to make the**S**e miceking**SSS** into a **SSS**tew!"

GREAT GROANING GLACIERS, THIS WAS REALLY THE END!

TAKE THE RATSLED!

The dragons continued to **argue** as Sizzle dangled Trap and Thea above a pool of **BOILING** water.

Bully's eyes narrowed. "Only Gobbler the Putrid can command u**S**. We don't take orders from anyone el**SSS**e!" he growled.

"I'll tell the king on you!" Sizzle shouted. He'll li**SSS**ten to me!"

"Don't threaten u**SSS**!" said Chomper.

"I've got an idea," **S**aid Bully. "Let'**SSS S**hare the miceking**SSS**! **SSS**o we can each **cook** one however we like."

FIRE shot from Sizzle's nostrils, missing my sister by half a **tail**!

"That **SSS**eeems fair to me," he said.

"Then let'**SSS** do thi**SSS**!" urged Bully. "I'm **SSS**o hungry I could eat a mountain of miceking**SSS**!"

I was still HIDDEN behind Chomper, paralyzed with fear — and from the **stench** of his scales.

"That'**SSS** not fair!" Chomper cried.

"Why not?" asked Sizzle.

"You don't know how to count," Chomper replied. "There are **two** miceking**SSS**, and **three** of u**SSS**!"

Sizzle counted on his claws. "He'**SSS** right. There are only **two** of them."

"Right! So we can't

Pull us up!

Help!

cook **ONE EACH**," said Chomper.

I knew Chomper was **lying** to the others. What would happen if they knew he was hiding me? I had a **guess**, but there was only one way to find out.

"That's not true. There are three micekings!" I **BRAVELY** cried out. "Chomper is **HIDING** me behind his back!"

"Chomper! You **TRAITOR**!" Sizzle fumed.

"Um . . . no, there's no **chubby** mouseking back here," Chomper said.

Sizzle **BONKED** Chomper on the head with his soup ladle.

"**LIAR!**" Sizzle cried. "That chubby mouseking i**SSS** under your tail!"

"Chomper! You **SSS**neak!" Bully said.

"Who are you calling a **SSS**neak?" Chomper yelled.

Then the three dragons began to **FIERCELY** fight one another, just as I had hoped! Sizzle **flung** Trap and Thea aside to free his claws, and they landed **safely** in a pile of sludge.

"Let's escape while they're distracted!" Thea cried.

We **FLED** the cave and ran back to the edge of the **mountain**. I looked **down,**

down,

down.

It was just a steep, icy wall.

"We can't get down from here!" I said.

"Don't be a scaredy-mouseking, Geronimo!" Thea scolded. "The dragons will **follow** us once they realize we've escaped."

"But it's too steep and icy!" I said.

"Don't worry. I've got a plan," said Trap.

"What kind of plan?" I asked him, my whiskers trembling. Anytime Trap had a plan, I usually ended up risking my fur!

He pointed to the big bundle on his back. "We'll try out my latest invention, the **ratsled**!"

He pulled two curved pieces of WOOD from his bag, along with some HOOKS, buckles, oiled rope, and half of a wooden BARREL. Then he worked quickly to put them together.

"This ratsled is just big enough to carry all

of us," he promised.

Then he handed wood **helmets** to me and Thea. "These will protect your **noggins**. Let's hop in and get going!"

"**NO, NO, NO!**" I protested. "I don't like your inventions. They never work!"

But Thea jumped right into the sled. "Let's give this a try!" she said **happily**.

"**TRUST ME**, Geronimo," Trap said. "Put on a **HELMET** and climb in."

THE RATSLED

A FASTER, BETTER SLED!

Trap's invention is fast and spacious! The curved wood rails permit the sled to glide at superspeeds. The safety cords secure equipment in the seating area. It's big enough to carry three micekings (depending on their sizes) and all passengers MUST wear a helmet.

I couldn't bring myself to do it. Knowing Trap, we would end up running into a **BOULDER**, or a **reiNDeer**, or a big TREE.

I could think of a *dozen* different ways that sled would make me *lose my fur*!

DOWN THE SLOPE!

"**HURRY UP**, Geronimo!" Trap urged as he climbed into the ratsled behind Thea. "We've got to *get moving*!"

But I was too scared. "Um, maybe we can think of another plan," I said.

Um...uh...

Get in!

Trap crossed his arms **impatiently** and glared at me. "Quit stalling, or else we'll all become **DRAGON FOOD**!"

"But the ratsled doesn't look **SAFE**," I protested.

"Come on, Geronimo," Trap coaxed me. "Aren't you **HUNGry**? Think about the **feast** that awaits us in the village. We'll celebrate with a banquet of **Stenchberg cheese** and pickled herrings. And Mousehilde will make us plenty of **gloog**!"

Thea joined in. "What are you waiting for? For herrings to jump out of their **bones** and into your mouth?"

Hearing them talk about food, I remembered that I was one **hungry mouseking**! I could almost smell the aroma of Stenchberg cheese. I held out my paw, as if I could grab a **CHUNK** out of the air. And then . . .

GUUUUUUUURGLE!

My stomach **erupted** in a rumble that was amplified by the walls of the mountain. It sounded like a **TERRIFYING** roar!

The racket roused the **EAGLES** from their nests. It interrupted the dragons' fight. And, worst of all, it caused an avalanche!

BOOOOOOOOOOMMMM!

Looking up at the very top of **EAGLES' CLIFF**, we could see an enormouse mound of snow **rolling** right toward us! Great groaning glaciers — that wasn't good!

"We're in **trouble** now!" Trap exclaimed.

Then the **dragons** burst out of the cave.

"Let'**SSS SSS**ee if they're **SSS**till here!"

"We'll gobble them up!"

"Let'**SSS** get tho**S**e rodent**SSS**!"

Shivering squids, we had to get out of there fast! So I jumped into the ratsled with a **MIGHTY** leap . . . and landed upside down in the seat!

"Hold on — we're leaving!" Thea called out.

Then the ratsled **took off** down the icy mountain, and I squealed in fright.

AAAAAAAAAAAAAH!

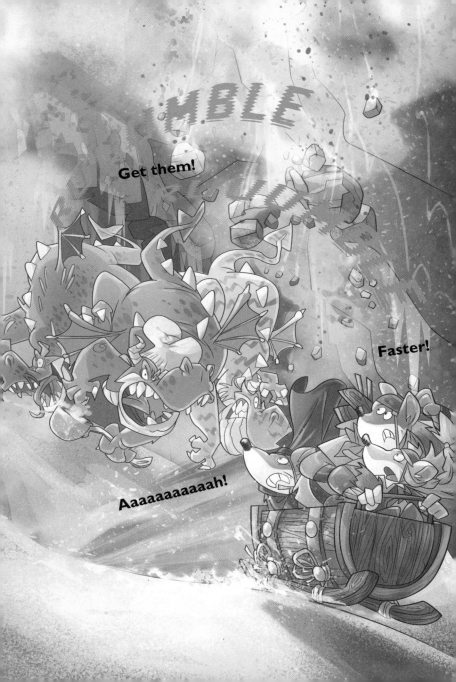

We **ZOOMED** down the slope at super-super-super-high speed, passing:

1 a pine forest. Thea maneuvered around the trees. Squeak! I was so scared.

2 a row of pointy rocks that beat up the bottom of the ratsled. Ow! My poor tail!

3 a deep icy crevasse, where we dodged curves, jumped over bumps, and made sharp turns. It made me ratsled-sick!

I'm getting worried!

Owie!

1

2

4   Finally, the crevasse ended with a bounce that launched us into the air at super-miceking speeds!

AAAAAAAAAAAAAAAH!"

The ratsled sailed **HIGH**, then **HIGHER**, then even **higher** . . . and then went down, down, **down**, diving into the Forest of a Thousand Scales.

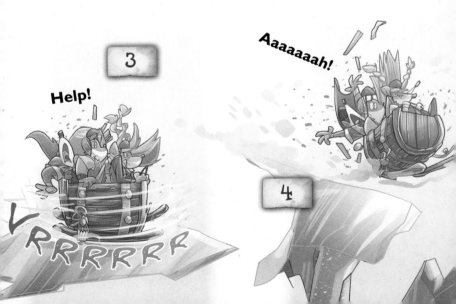

Luckily, THEA was a skilled pilot! She bounced from BRANCH to BRANCH until we reached the coast.

When I finally opened my eyes, we were SLIDING in the direction of the *Bated Breath*, which was just a few yards away. The ratsled SCREECHED to a halt — and then broke into pieces!

"The ratsled did great!" Trap said proudly.

Olaf called out from the ship. "All hands on

What a great invention!

deck, you squishy slugs! We leave immediately!"

"That means you, too, *GERONIMO*," he added. **"YOU LAZY CHEESEHEAD!"**

Get a move on!

Hurry up!

Come on!

DRAGON ATTACK!

We **set sail** immediately, taking advantage of the favorable winds. I grabbed an oar and started rowing to help us along.

"Geronimo, are the **DRAGONS** following us?" Olaf called out to me.

I **SQUINTED** at the horizon behind us — and saw **SIZZLE**, **BULLY**, and **CHOMPER** flying right toward us!

"They're on our tail!" I cried out.

OLAF shook his paw. "Row faster, everyone, if you don't want to be gobbled up like **CODFISH**!"

As we sailed into the port of Mouseborg, we heard the dragon alarm ring out from Lookout Cliff.

TOOT-TOOOOOOOOT!
TOOT-TOOOOOOOOT!

Sven the Shouter ran to meet us. "Did you find the **wild mint**?" he asked.

Trap held up the plants. "**Mission accomplished!**"

Then Sven saw the three flying reptiles. "Who told you cheeseheads to bring back the dragons, too?"

We didn't answer, because we were

busy **running** for cover like the rest of the micekings. We dashed inside the **RED HERRING**, the village diner, just as the dragons **DESCENDED** on the village.

They spewed flames from their nostrils.

"Look at all the ta**SSS**ty miceking**SSS**!" said Sizzle.

"And they're all for u**SSS**!" added Bully.

"You can gobble up the other one**S**, but the chubby mou**S**eking is all mine," said Chomper. "When I **SSS**ee him, I'll fry him in a flash!"

Sven began to shout orders.

"Load the catapults! Get ready to launch!"

But we couldn't load the catapults with heavy boulders. **Great groaning glaciers**, they were full of **snow**!

Sizzle began to dive-bomb the village

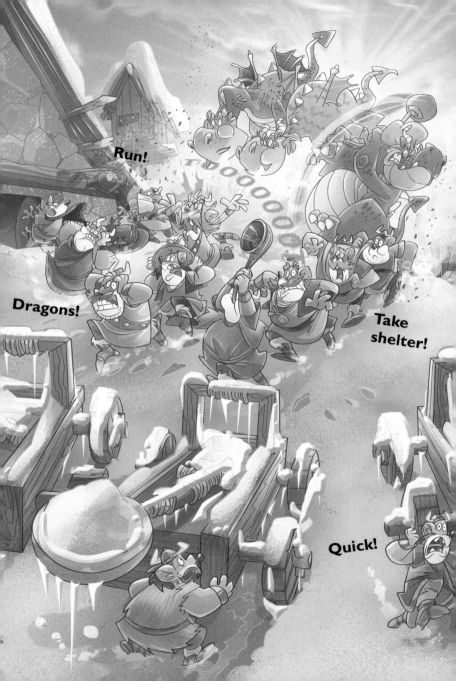

streets, trying to smack fleeing micekings with his soup ladle! Panicked rodents ran from him as fast as they could.

Thea looked me right in the eye. "Geronimo, we must do something. The village is in trouble and it's our fault."

I knew she was right, but I was still afraid. "B-b-but, they're shooting flames! What can we do? Arm ourselves with snowballs?"

Thea smirked. "That's just silly," she said. Then she froze. "Wait a minute, maybe it's not so silly. You said snowballs, right, Geronimo? That's an icetastic idea!"

"What? Really?" I asked.

"Fill those buckets with WATER, quickly!" Thea ordered. "Trap, come help us!"

Thea had Trap and me carry buckets to the catapults and dump ICY WATER on the snow. That turned the piles of **snow** filling the catapults into **DANGEROUS** balls of **ice**. How clever! The other micekings saw us and started copying us.

Sven gave a great shout:

"*Ready! Aim! Fire! Fire! Fire!*"

The unexpected rain of ice balls took the three dragons by **surprise**. It **COOLED**

This should work!

down their fiery attacks. They zigged and zagged to avoid the ice.

Then . . . **BAM**! One ball hit Sizzle on the nose and he fell into the freezing water of the fjord.

Everyone knows that dragons hate **cold** water, and they especially hate it when it's **clean**!

"Retreat, fa**sss**t!" Sizzle hissed. "I must find a pool of hot, **sss**tinky water. I'm freezing!"

The dragons flew off, shaking their long, **SCALY** tails behind them.

"Scram, dragons!" Sven **SHOUTED**. "You won't get any miceking meat this winter. So says Sven the Shouter!"

"SO SAYS SVEN THE SHOUTER!" cheered the micekings.

WHERE'S MY MICEKING HELMET?

A little beaten up, but with our fur safe and sound, we handed the **wild mint** to our village chief.

Sven gave a triumphant shout:

"People of Mouseborg, rejoice! They have found the wild mint! Mousehilde will conquer her cold!"

The micekings of the village rewarded us with **thunderous** applause.

"As is our tradition, we will *celebrate* the end of this battle with a banquet fit for a barbarian!" Sven added. "We will stuff ourselves like **POLAR BEARS**! We will drink **barrels** of finnbrew! And Mousehilde will make her mousetastic **gloog**!"

Thora rushed off to prepare the wild mint tea for her mother.

"LONG LIVE SVEN THE SHOUTER!" everyone cheered.

So we celebrated Mousehilde's recovery and our unexpected **victory** in that **WINTER** battle.

After a triple serving of gloog, my stomach finally stopped frightening the micekings with its wild **GURGLINGS**. Suddenly, I remembered what **Sven** had said before our journey.

He had promised me my very own **MICEKING HELMET**! Finally! At long, long last, I had done it. **THORA** might finally start to **LOOK** at me as if I were a real mouseking!

Who knows? I thought. ***Maybe*** . . . *she will even smile at me!*

So I approached Sven. "I am ready, my valiant chief!" I said **SOLEMNLY**.

"Ready for what, SMARTY-MOUSEKING?" Sven asked.

"Ready to receive from you our greatest honor," I replied. "A miceking helmet!"

Sven snickered at first, and then an angry look crossed his face. "You brought the dragons *right to our village* in the middle of winter, and you want a reward? Forget it!"

"Not even a tiny helmet?" I protested weakly. "That's not fair."

I sighed. Luckily, my nephew BENJAMIN was there to lift my spirits.

He must have noticed my SAD EXPRESSION.

"Even without a miceking helmet, Uncle, you're my hero," he said.

And then he jumped into my arms. Thea and Trap joined the GROUP HUG.

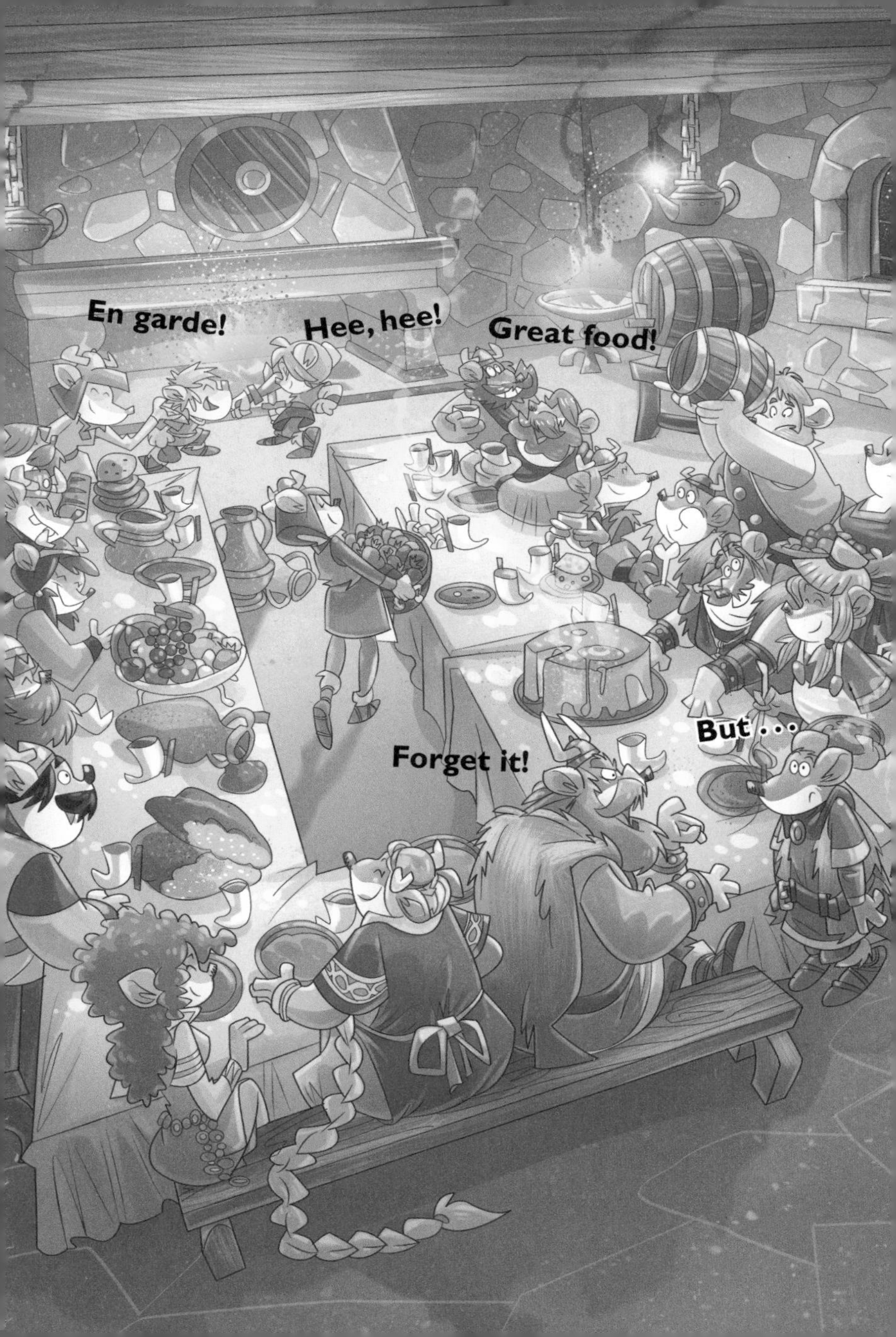
En garde!
Hee, hee!
Great food!
Forget it!
But . . .

"One day you'll get the helmet," Thea promised.

Trap **SMiLED**. "Meanwhile, instead of a **miceking** helmet, you can wear a **RATSLED** helmet. What do you say, cousin?"

You're our hero!

You'll get one!

I love you!

Ah, that's the Stiltonord way!

A united **FAMILY** like mine will always be the greatest reward any rodent could wish for! And who knows, maybe one day I really will have my own miceking helmet . . .

BUT THAT'S ANOTHER MICEKING STORY FOR ANOTHER DAY!

Want to read the next adventure of the micekings? I can't wait to tell you all about it!

THE FAMOUSE FJORD RACE

It's the day of the Famouse Fjord Race, the miceking competition to determine the best sailormouse. Geronimo Stiltonord isn't competing, since he's not a sailormouse at all . . . but then he's dragged into a boat! Just when he thinks things can't get worse, the mice learn that the dragons are preparing for another attack. Squeak!

Be sure to read all my fabumouse adventures!

#1 Lost Treasure of the Emerald Eye

#2 The Curse of the Cheese Pyramid

#3 Cat and Mouse in a Haunted House

#4 I'm Too Fond of My Fur!

#5 Four Mice Deep in the Jungle

#6 Paws Off, Cheddarface!

#7 Red Pizzas for a Blue Count

#8 Attack of the Bandit Cats

#9 A Fabumouse Vacation for Geronimo

#10 All Because of a Cup of Coffee

#11 It's Halloween, You 'Fraidy Mouse!

#12 Merry Christmas, Geronimo!

#13 The Phantom of the Subway

#14 The Temple of the Ruby of Fire

#15 The Mona Mousa Code

#16 A Cheese-Colored Camper

#17 Watch Your Whiskers, Stilton!

#18 Shipwreck on the Pirate Islands

#19 My Name Is Stilton, Geronimo Stilton

#20 Surf's Up, Geronimo!

#21 The Wild, Wild West

#22 The Secret of Cacklefur Castle

A Christmas Tale

#23 Valentine's Day Disaster

#24 Field Trip to Niagara Falls

#25 The Search for Sunken Treasure

#26 The Mummy with No Name

#27 The Christmas Toy Factory

#28 Wedding Crasher

#29 Down and Out Down Under

#30 The Mouse Island Marathon

#31 The Mysterious Cheese Thief

Christmas Catastrophe

#32 Valley of the Giant Skeletons

#33 Geronimo and the Gold Medal Mystery

#34 Geronimo Stilton, Secret Agent

#35 A Very Merry Christmas

#36 Geronimo's Valentine

#37 The Race Across America

#38 A Fabumouse School Adventure

#39 Singing Sensation

#40 The Karate Mouse

#41 Mighty Mount Kilimanjaro

#42 The Peculiar Pumpkin Thief

#43 I'm Not a Supermouse!

#44 The Giant Diamond Robbery

#45 Save the White Whale!

#46 The Haunted Castle

#47 Run for the Hills, Geronimo!

#48 The Mystery in Venice

#49 The Way of the Samurai

#50 This Hotel Is Haunted!

#51 The Enormouse Pearl Heist

#52 Mouse in Space!

#53 Rumble in the Jungle

#54 Get into Gear, Stilton!

#55 The Golden Statue Plot

#56 Flight of the Red Bandit

Special Edition!
The Hunt for the Golden Book

#57 The Stinky Cheese Vacation

#58 The Super Chef Contest

#59 Welcome to Moldy Manor

Special Edition!
The Hunt for the Curious Cheese

#60 The Treasure of Easter Island

#61 Mouse House Hunter

#62 Mouse Overboard!

Special Edition!
The Hunt for the Secret Papyrus

#63 The Cheese Experiment

Join me and my friends as we travel through time in these very special editions!

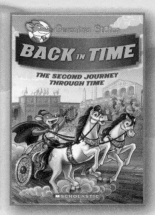

THE JOURNEY THROUGH TIME

BACK IN TIME: THE SECOND JOURNEY THROUGH TIME

THE RACE AGAINST TIME: THE THIRD JOURNEY THROUGH TIME

Dear mouse friends,
thanks for reading,

and good-bye until
the next book!